Countdown to Summer:

A Poem for Every Day of the School Year

COUNTDOWN TO SUMMER:
A POEM FOR EVERY DAY OF THE SCHOOL YEAR

by J. PATRICK LEWIS
illustrations by
ETHAN LONG

LITTLE, BROWN AND COMPANY
Books for Young Readers
New York   Boston

Little, Brown Books for Young Readers

Hachette Book Group
237 Park Avenue, New York, NY 10017
Visit our Web site at www.lb-kids.com

First Edition: July 2009

Little, Brown Books for Young Readers is a division of Hachette Book Group, Inc.
The Little, Brown name and logo are trademarks of Hachette Book Group, Inc.

ISBN 978-0-316-02089-3

10 9 8 7 6 5 4 3 2 1

RRD-C

Printed in the United States of America

The illustrations for this book were drawn with a Faber Castell, Schwartz Black,
non-graphite pencil on Strathmore 400 Series Medium Drawing paper.
The text was set in Whitney and the display type is TFMaltbyAntique.
Numerals are set in Flyer and title type is set in CongressSans.

Acknowledgements

My deepest thanks to the anthologists and magazine/journal editors who generously published some of the poems that follow: the late Myra Cohn Livingston, Lee Bennett Hopkins, Paul B. Janeczko, Georgia Heard, X.J. Kennedy and Dorothy Kennedy, Jack Prelutsky, Jane Yolen, Bobbi Katz, Eric Kimmel, Ralph Fletcher, John Foster, Andrew Fusek Peters, Cindy Kane, *Cricket, Light Quarterly, Journal of Children's Literature, Bookbird, Language Arts, Reading Today, Book Links,* and *Elysian Fields Quarterly.*

For Beth, Matt, and Leigh Ann

With love,
JPL

A Sixth Grader Sees the Future

In a billion years, A.D.,
Our sun will shine for none to see.
The sea will miss each passing ship;
The sky will hover over zip.
Those blazing stars will start to cool,
And I won't have to go to school.

In a billion years from now—
Or maybe more—but anyhow,
The earth may shrivel up and die.
The universe? Pi in the sky.
The future, spinning, may have spun.
And I might have my homework done.

Button-Down Bill

Button-down Bill
Had buttons a-plenty.
He buttoned his buttons
Where he didn't have any.
He buttoned his shoes,
His pants and coat,
He buttoned his buttons
Till he buttoned his throat.
He buttoned his lips,
His ears and nose,
He buttoned his head
Like he buttoned his clothes!
He buttoned his kids
And he buttoned his wife.
"Button up!" said Bill,
All his buttoned-down life.
So if you should hear
A buttoned-up shout,
That's button-down Bill . . .

Pllzzzz! Lt me ouutt!

Gold Teeth

I put a tooth under my pillow
And got a quarter. I was four.

And now I'm five. I put two teeth
Under my pillow. I got more.

If I keep losing teeth like this,
The Tooth Fairy will come again,

And when she stops I won't be mad
'Cause I'll be rich when I am ten.

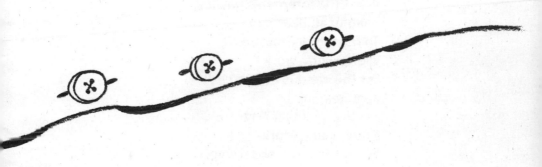

Work, Work, Work

Wake, wake, wake
For the day's beginning,
Think, think, think,
An idea's spinning.
Turn, turn, turn,
The machines are charging,
Push, push, push
For the barges barging.
Drive, drive, drive
What the trucks are hauling,
Hear, hear, hear
What the foreman's bawling.
Beat, beat, beat
To the factory humming,
Work, work, work
For the night is coming.
Rest, rest, rest
For the all-deserving,
Mark, mark, mark,
What the day's observing.

Home Poem
Or, the Sad
Dog Song

Home of the fly: pie.

Home of the frog: log.

Home of the bear: lair.

Home of the gnu: zoo.

Home of the bee: tree.

Home of the mole: hole.

Home of the ants: pants.

Home of the moth: cloth.

Home of the otter: water.

Home of the shark: dark.

Home of the snake: lake.

Home of the moose: spruce.

Home of the flea: me!

Reading *Harry Potter* Under the Sheets

I'm quarter-past Chapter One
Of the last of Harry's feats.
This flashlight's my midnight sun.
I burrow under the sheets.

Book Seven's supposed to be
The last of the Rowling run.
Gazillions can't wait to see
Who's defeated and who's won.

Will Voldemort get his due?
Will Ron or Hermione die?
Or Hagrid? Is Hagrid through?
Now who will it be and why?

Which one of the villains meets
His death by the hero foe?
I burrow under the sheets.
By the weekend I should know.

The Librarian

After school one day I was talking to Mr.
Butterwinkle, the school librarian.
"**C**an you
Define ABECEDARIAN?" I asked.
"**E**asy," he said. "But
First I think *you* should
Go to Webster's Unabridged Dictionary, and . . .
Hmm, here's one," he said. "Now,
Isabelle, when you're looking for sparkling word
Jewels, try to
Keep them spit-shined, ready to go. A dictionary's
Like a trap, an irresistible
Mind trap
No one wants to escape from.
Once you discover one beaut—
P*oof!*—up pop two more fifty-cent
Quality words in
Rapid
Succession,
Totally
Unexpected
Verbal
Whizbangs.
Xerox them. Hang them in your locker. Now
You're in the
Zone. Oh, I forgot. ABECEDARIAN. Look it up."

Book Etiquette

Be kind and gentle to the Book
   Called *Frog and Toad Are Friends*
Or *Peter Pan (and Captain Hook)*
   Or *Where the Sidewalk Ends,*
The Chronicles of Narnia
   Or *Where the Red Fern Grows.*
A Book has so much character,
   As every reader knows.

Oh, do not make a dog-ear when
   A Bookmark can be used
And never tear a page—a Book
   Dislikes being abused.
Trite scribbles in the margin can
   Set off a Book's alarm.
How would you like *"Puh-leeze!"* or *"Bull's eye!"*
   Tattoed on your arm?

So read a Book and put it back
   With care upon the shelf.
Remember not to put it where
   You wouldn't sit yourself.

(P.S. Just kidding! Every Book
   Would love to be the rage
And get its chapters dirty till
   The ink's read off the page!)

172 Eid ul-Fitr*

The new moon is rising.
Ramadan has passed,
Holiest of holy months
When true believers fast.

Gathering at the mosque,
Borne on wings of prayer,
Quitting fast to feast,
A festival affair,

Muslims know the way
Of sacrifice. They kneel
And bow in humbled awe.
At Eid the faithful feel

Such piety and peace
That brothers end their feuds,
And mothers keep their joy
Wrapped in gratitude.

*Muslim holiday beginning on the
day after the month of Ramadan

Me Irish Grandmother Flynn

I loved her I did, I loved her,
Me Irish Grandmother Flynn.
When she died and they put her away in a
grave . . .
"I wouldn't," she said,
"No, I couldn't," she said,
So she didn't,
She *didn't* stay in.

They spied her they did, they spied her
Flying low over Pittsburgh town.
But whenever they tried to get her inside . . .
"I couldn't," she said,
"No, I shouldn't," she said,
So she didn't,
She *didn't* come down.

I coaxed her I did, I coaxed her,
But me Irish Grandmother flew
Up and around Pencil Vani-a-ha!
"If I ever," she said,
"But I'll never," she said,
"For there's *ever*
So *much* left to do!"

170 Dead Weight

Everyone knew that
He was rich and fat,
But no one ever learned
How much he urned.

169 The Poet of the World

"How ho-ho-hum has the planet become!"
   Cried the Poet of the World.
"I must sonnet the wind, sestina the sea."
   Then he dipped his pen and he swirled

Out a poem where braves become braver, and knaves
   Wander under a vinegar sky,
And a Duchess receives purely innocent thieves
   Who are normally camera shy.

"The heroes are villains, the geniuses mad!"
   So he spun them a roundelay.
"All the people who live in the Ivory Land
   Would be happier villanelle gray."

Then he thought, "I must metaphor girls in gold
   And simile boys in blue."
He looked up from his Book, and he said, "I forgot,
   Which character are you?"

168 Werewolf

Once legend ran
    Across the gulf
Of truth: A man
    Became a wolf

Quite helplessly
    By shifting shape
At Moonrise. He
    Made his escape

To howl and lurk
    With dripping fangs—
Then went berserk!
    And thereby hangs

The savage tale
    Of one poor lad
Whose bloody trail
    Drove him quite mad

For what occurred—
    The lunar pull—
Is not absurd:
    The Moon was full.

167 Wet September

The Grasshopper swaying
in the rain
on a spear of wheat
held fast . . .

Is like a distant
ship captain,
sea swept
against the mast.

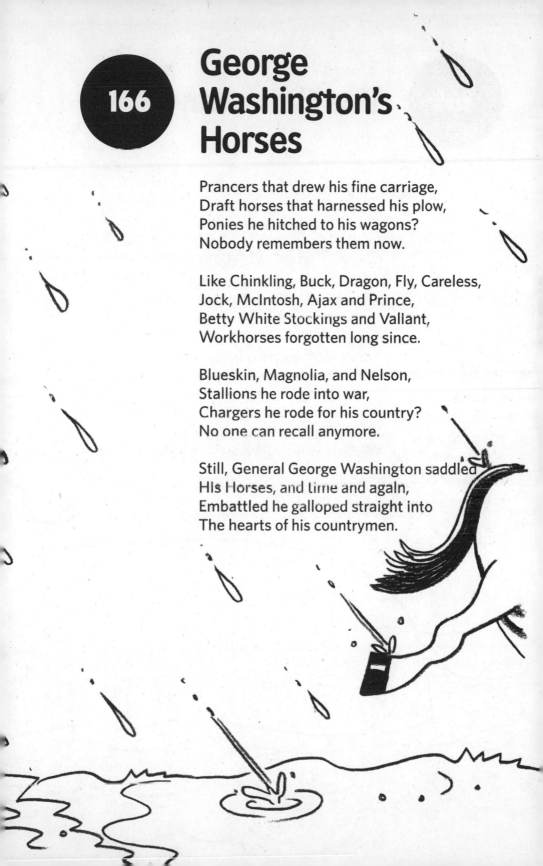

George Washington's Horses

Prancers that drew his fine carriage,
Draft horses that harnessed his plow,
Ponies he hitched to his wagons?
Nobody remembers them now.

Like Chinkling, Buck, Dragon, Fly, Careless,
Jock, McIntosh, Ajax and Prince,
Betty White Stockings and Vallant,
Workhorses forgotten long since.

Blueskin, Magnolia, and Nelson,
Stallions he rode into war,
Chargers he rode for his country?
No one can recall anymore.

Still, General George Washington saddled
His Horses, and time and again,
Embattled he galloped straight into
The hearts of his countrymen.

165 The Hathaways

Alexander Hathaway
Couldn't clear a path away,
Which is why he loved being a twin,

For he mixed his dirty clothes
With his sister's nerdy clothes
And he had her room to dump them in!

Angelina Hathaway
Was a soothing bath away
From rereading *Huckleberry Finn*,

When her brother sneaked a peek!
Now he's grounded for a week,
Which is why *she* loves being a twin.

Barnaby Butterby Bitter III
(The Bookaphobic Hippo)

"I never read books, I never need books!"
Said Barnaby Butterby Bitter III.
"It should be a crime, this wasting of time
With tedious, toadious reading. My word!"

But several years passed disarmingly fast
For Barnaby Butterby Bitter III.
And one day he found that only the sound
Of his utterly Bitterly voice could be heard!

So he picked up a book (though he shivered and shook)
And Barnaby Butterby Bitter III
Went on to discover from cover to cover
The happy, the sappy, the mad and absurd

Delight of the ages in thirty-two pages!
So Barnaby Butterby Bitter III
Cruised down the lagoon with *Goodnight Moon*.
Hippo-notized as he re-re-re-re-
Re-reread every goodnight word!

163 I Was Your Teacher Once

I was your teacher once. You may remember me.
I am the chalk dust of memory.
I was the trusted ship you sailed.
You were the promise I unveiled.
I was the show. You were the tell.
I was your magic. You were my spell.
I was the ticket. You were the game.
I was the candle. You were the flame.
I was the curtain. You were the play.
I was the sculptor. You were the clay.
I was your teacher once. You may remember me.

162 So I've Been Told

There was an old lady, a hundredfold.
I don't know how she got so old.
Just because, so I've been told.

She flossed her teeth and brushed them twice,
Upon her dentist's good advice.
She polished her teeth to shine like gold.
I don't know how she got so old.
Just because, so I've been told.

She spit-and-polished her Sunday shoes
So well she didn't know which to choose.
She polished her shoes to shine like teeth,
She polished her teeth to shine like gold.
I don't know how she got so old.
Just because, so I've been told.

She lifted the rugs to polish the floors
Of fifteen rooms and the corridors.
She polished the floors to shine like shoes,
She polished her shoes to shine like teeth,
She polished her teeth to shine like gold.
I don't know how she got so old.
Just because, so I've been told.

She stopped the chimes to polish the clocks,
She shined the Ticks and shined the Tocks.
She polished the clocks to shine like floors,
She polished the floors to shine like shoes,
She polished her shoes to shine like teeth,
She polished her teeth to shine like gold.
I don't know how she got so old.
Just because, so I've been told.

She sprayed and waxed and polished the car—
You'd think it belonged to a movie star!
She polished the car to shine like clocks,
She polished the clocks to shine like floors,
She polished the floors to shine like shoes,
She polished her shoes to shine like teeth,
She polished her teeth to shine like gold.
I don't know how she got so old.
Just because, so I've been told.

She polished all day and polished all night
Till every last thing was spiffy and bright,
Which polished her off, and the reason was—
I've been told it was . . . just because.

To eBay

To eBay, to eBay, to buy baby diapers,
Tweezers and freezers and windshield wipers,
Q-tips, a bulldozer, shoes you adore,
Unexplored parts of New Jersey, and more!
To eBay, to eBuy impossible dreams,
To eBay, to eBuy, how wondrous it seems.

Old Queen Cole

Old Queen Cole
Was a very old troll,
And they bury old trolls, you see;
She called for her coffin,
And she called for a hole,
In a sanitary cemeter-ee!
They brought that coffin, but just to soften
The spot where a Queen should be
They put down a Pamper in a clean
   clothes hamper
Reserved for Her Royalty.
And they buried her deep
So the Queen could sleep
In her underwear. . . . *Pardon me!*

159 A Gecko's Neck

The echo from a gecko
Is an echo never heard
For if you check his neck, a gecko,
Heck, can't say a word.

But wait a sec, if you inspect a
Gecko's neck, I've heard,
Expect a peck of gecko peck-a-
Pecks just like a bird.

158 There Was an Old Woman

There was an old woman
Who lived in a sneaker.
She had so many Keds
Her life was getting bleaker.

She tied their shoelaces
Together for fun,
And now those poor Keds
Have nowhere to run.

The Turrible Troll

The turrible turrible Troll decided
   He would gobble John,
A lowly knave, and from his cave
   With Trollish trousers on

Yelled, "Give me a sip and then a nip
   Of Shetland tea and thee!"
Young John ran faster farther faster
   Than the Troll could see.

The Troll sat down and waited
   As around the forest ran
Young John. The hurrible hurrible Troll
   Played catch-him-as-you-can.

A third of a third of a day went by,
   And peeking round a tree,
The Troll said, "Halley-McGalliganish!
   Young John's returned to me."

The days will get much shorter now,
   The evenings get much colder.
But I fear poor Young John will not
   Be getting any older.

156

Weather in a Word: *Still*

There is no weather
On the Moon—
No wind or sound,
No snow or rain.
Inside is out
If you are peeking
Through a lunar
Windowpane.

Breathless days
Of blistering heat,
Nights blanketed
With bitter cold
Leave the silence
Undisturbed
And the climate
Uncontrolled.

155 Riddle

What begins with Y
And ends with Y
And is long gone now?
Good-bye.

154 The Wedding of the Lion and the Mouse on Vacation from the Sandy Eggo Zoo

The lion took the wedding ring—
  A Frosted Cheerio—
And placed it on the mouse's paw
  But delicately so.
She nibbled at it, then she said,
  "You are my Roameo."

The lion wore a tiger tux
  And cummerbund, the rogue.
The mouse's dress? A tea cozy
  She'd read about in *Vogue*.

Six shiny crawdad bridesmaids wore
  Six toilet paper veils.
A pelican, the best man, led
  Six slimy usher snails.

The rabbit was a Rabbi
  (If you take away the "t")
For weddings are exactly where
  A Rabbi ought to be.

"A raisin toast," the Rabbi said,
  "To Abigail, the bride,
And blushing lion-hearted
  Alexander by her side."

But when the lion roared, the mouse
  Squeaked back, and you just knew,
Two sounds were never sweeter
  Than "I DO!" and then "Me, too!"—
About 4,000 miles from
  The Sandy Eggo Zoo.

153 Victor Predictor

Victor Predictor points up in the air.
Victor predicts by the Weatherman's prayer:
  "Rain. Could be snow.
  Maybe sun? All I know—"
Says Victor Predictor, "it comes from up there."

152 Crackers

There once lived a Baron of Rottenham Green,
A slightly cracked egg of a fellow.
His hair was purple,
His eyes were red,
His ears were blue,
Likewise his head,
And his teeth were sunshine yellow.

He knitted his name on the national flag
Stuffed in a soup tureen,
The snick-snack name,
The crackerjack name,
The plump pumpernickel and tickle-us name
Of Baron McCarran O'Knickerbock Nolliver
Oliver Bland Saltine.

"Never address me," he said with a grin,
"As Nolly or Ollie-be-good
Or Rotten or Nicky His Crackership,
Is that perfectly understood?

"And as for you, my dear," said he
To the Lady of Rottenham Green,
"As his lordship, I have already banned
Nolly and Ollie,
Especially, by golly,
Nicky His Crackership, Esquire.
Do you think you understand?"

The Lady of Rottenham Green tut-tutted,
"Because, my dearest fellow,
Your hair is purple,
Your eyes are red,
Your ears are blue
And so's your head,
And your teeth are mustard yellow.
Your nose is long,
Your pants are short,
According to Rottenham's
Fashion Report.
Your manners are dull,
Your brain is small,
And besides it's full
Of nothing at all,
Is it any wonder I think I shall call you . . .

"Hmmmm,
Let me see . . .
Not Nicky or Nolly
Or Rotten or Ollie—
Nothing so happy or melancholy.
There must be a name, a crackerjack name
Somewhere in between . . .
A name that reveals
How everyone feels—
I've got it! I think I have got it! You are
His Perfectly Bland Saltine."

151 Ms. Penelope P. Potts: Fire Station Dalmatian

Without a fire, a fireman has little else to do.
So firemen feeling rather bored at Station 22
Made up a number game that's known as "Guess How Many Spots."
The subject of the game was Ms. Penelope P. Potts.

Penelope, Penelope, the Fire House Dalmatian,
Puzzled (though she nuzzled up to) this red fire station.
Her multitude of furry spots did not approach infinity,
Though Orville Higgenloopler said, "It's up in that vicinity."

José O'Leary claimed it's all in density and mass,
Nemiah Ping preferred to use a magnifying glass.
"Nineteen!" one bellowed. "Forty-nine!" "Ten thousand eighty-three!"
The only one who knew for sure was Ms. Penelope.

The closest guess? The Fire Chief Renaldo Babblejack
Had almost yelled, "I've got it!" but he suddenly lost track
And started counting over till long after it was dark:
Counting doggie dots is not a picnic in the park.

The fire alarm went off, and all the firemen climbed aboard.
The hook and ladder rumbled out; the fire hoses poured.
And as the crew of 22 had doused the raging blaze,
The Polka-Dotted Counted Countess held her haughty gaze.

Returning to the station, not one fireman could think
Who wrote the Post-it note cemented to the kitchen sink.
It read: "Of dots there are, my friends, one hundred twenty-three!"
Beneath it was a signature in paw print: "P.P.P."

150 Oogalie Boogalie Boo!

Their eyes are dead as coffin holes,
Their bodies thin as fishing poles,
Their whispers leave you wide awake
Because the only sound they make
  Is *Oogalie Boogalie Boo!*

They come in threes, they come in twos,
And leave long pearly curlicues
That ooze into your every dream
Accompanied by frightful scream
  Of *Oogalie Boogalie Boo!*

Each *Boo!* assumes a spooky shape.
If only there were some escape. . . .
Kidnipping's brought them so much fame,
And yet they have no other name
  Than *Oogalie Boogalie Boo!*

I saw one sleeping on the swing.
I tiptoed past the ugly thing,
But just before I reached the door,
I heard the terrifying roar
  Of *Oogalie Boogalie Boo!*

They follow children home from school.
They caught one daydreaming, the fool!
No one has seen the poor boy since!
But *someone's* left his fingerprints—
  An *Oogalie Boogalie Boo!*

A Lasting Impression

I scratched your initials
on the seat of my chair—
now you're stuck
on my underwear!

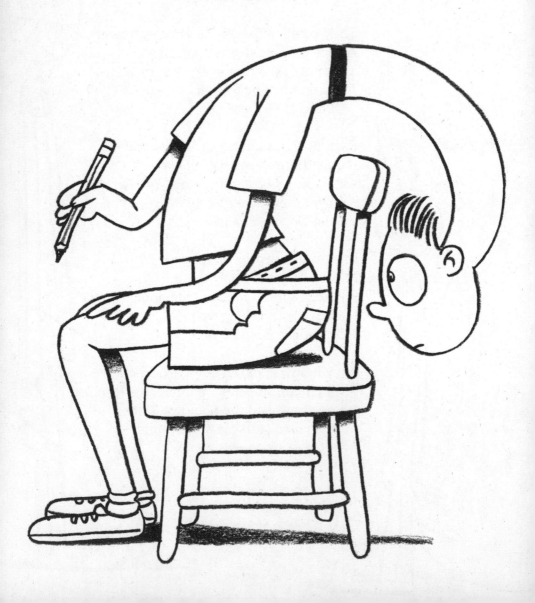

Over the Ocean Blue

Isabella, Isabella,
Ferdinand, Ferdinand.
Christopher, Christopher, you

Received three ships
From the King and Queen
In 1492.

Asia, Asia,
India, India—
Lands you thought you knew

Turned out to be
San Salvador
With a New World ocean view.

A frantic Atlantic,
Bahama sea drama!
Christopher, Christopher, two

Hip-hips for the trips
In the sailing ships,
To the captain and his crew.

Dolly and Dilly

Dolly and Dilly
Were sister and bro.
Everywhere Dolly went,
Dilly would go.
Everywhere Dilly went,
Dolly would not.
"Dilly," said Dolly,
"I must have forgot."

Dilly and Dolly
Were brother and sis.
Everything Dolly did
Dilly would miss.
Everything Dolly did
Dilly would say,
"Dolly forgot me
Again today."

In a Book I Once Read

The Chicken's Song

In a book I once read as a chick-chick-chick
(Said the Duke to himself, said he)
I learned that a Rooster is only a trick
(Said the Duke to himself, said he).
So I stuck out my chin, then I puffed up my chest,
Allowing my *back* end to do all the rest,
And I thought to myself, I'm the best of the best
(Said the Duke to himself, said he).

I *look* like a Rooster, the Cock of the Walk
(Said the Duke to himself, said he).
And when I'm parading, the Chickens all gawk
(Said the Duke to himself, said he).
But the lesson I learned as a chick, I'm afraid,
Was impossibly wrong! The mistake that I made
Was when I discovered the *EGG* that I'd laid!
(Said the Duchess herself, said she.)

The Colossal Octopus

Now the Kraken was a baddy,
The Gargantuan granddaddy
  Of the monsters of the sea.
And when he would meet a sailor
On a rowboat, yacht, or whaler,
He would turn him so much paler
  Than a sailor ought to be.

Well, from Norroway to Thailand,
They mistook him for an island—
  He was near a mile wide.
When the sea began a-buzzin',
It was crazy Kraken, cousin,
With those arms, at least a dozen,
  And some armlets on the side.

Took a frigate, scrubbed and washed it
None too gently, then he squashed it
  Into tiny cabinetry.
And from summer into autumn,
Kraken gurgled, "Zzookle-klottum!"
As he sat upon his bottom
  On the bottom of the sea.

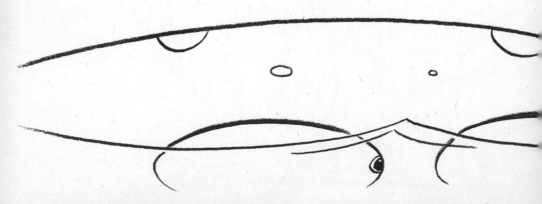

The Dragonfly

Lit flittingly
On window-wings
Beside a bee
To ponder things

Such as, *Why
Is the wind a wind?*
"Becuzz, becuzz,"
Buzzed Velvet-skinned.

*Why does the sky
Pretend it's gray?
Who painted mountain-
tops that way?
Who thought up mud,
Invented showers?*

"What bzzzzness, Bud,
Is that of ours?"

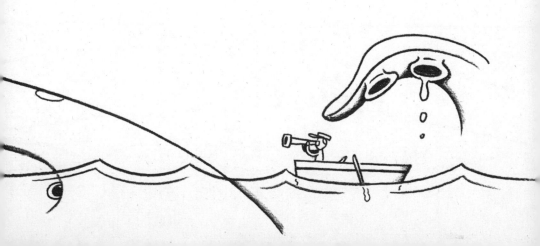

143

Proposed Amendment to the Constitution

The President and Vice-President of the United States shall be required to take the Fourth Grade Standardized Achievement Test so that **No President or Vice-President shall be left behind.**

142 Twitt, Skinner, and Corn

He's General Twitt, alligator-mean,
He can whup three sides of a square marine,
So they put him in charge of the putting green,
The tee and the cup and the in-between!
  Hut-hut, hut-hut, hut-hut!

He's Private Skinner of the Infantry.
Says, "Where do they put whiz kids like me?
With the brains I've got, why, I bet I'll be
Potato Skinner of the Company!"
  Hut-hut, hut-hut, hut-hut!

He's Colonel Corn of the Signal Corps.
Sends messages by two-by-four.
He can't quite figure out the score—
They call for Peace, he signals WAR!
  Hut-hut, hut-hut, hut-hut!

What Is Earth?

What is earth, whale?
A sea where I sing.
What is earth, robin?
A thing I call Spring.
What is earth, python?
A space to squeeze in.
What is earth, penguin?
A place to freeze in.
What is earth, camel?
A land without water.
What is earth, housefly?
No spot for a swatter.
What is earth, earthworm?
An apple a day.
What is earth, groundhog?
A hole in PA.
What is earth, eagle?
A sky where I soar.
What is earth, cockroach?
A house I explore.
What is earth, eel?
It's really quite shocking.
What is earth, snail?
Where I go out walking
What is earth, parrot?
Where I am still talking
  and talking
  and talking
  and talking. . . .

The Dreamer

As Augie McNaughton got ready for school,
    A full moon caught his eye.
He stared at it far too long, and soon
    The school bus passed him by.

Then Augie McNaughton ran so fast
    That he got to school by eight,
And he told his teacher, Mrs. O'Toole,
    That the moon had made him late.

She gave him a book with a knowing look
    And said, "You will be amazed!"
As he read *The Skies Above*, he dreamed
    In an Augie McNaughton haze.

When Augie McNaughton returned from school,
    Aunt Maude asked what he'd been taught.
"I learned about space," Augie said. "Can you picture
    Me as an astronaut?"

And Augie McNaughton grew and grew
    With a faraway look in his eyes. . . .
I saw him once in a rocket ship
    That soared across the skies.

The Cellar

Who heard the scream and then the moan?
The cellar's made of cold, cold stone.
I won't go down those stairs alone
   With *my* imagination.

The people who lit out from here
Before us said, *What's there to fear?*
Your cellar ghosts rarely appear.
   It's my imagination?

I asked the neighbor what he'd heard
But he gave me his solemn word,
The moaning hasn't reoccurred.
   It's your imagination.

Rickety stairs, too long, too steep,
Consume the lantern light I sweep
Over the chasm of a deep
   Cave: my imagination.

I swear I heard it pierce the night,
A sound that slashed the dark, and white
Phantasms scarving out of sight . . .
   Of my imagination.

You're Pretty...

Your pretty mouth,
Your pretty chin,
Your pretty face,
Your pretty skin.

Your pretty ears,
Your pretty nose,
Your pretty teeth
In pretty rows.

Your pretty hair,
Your pretty skull,
My pretty, you
Are pretty dull.

137 Do Not Let the Goblins In!

They live fast,
Die young,
Love the night,
Hate the sun.
If you let
The Goblins in,
Their skunky smell
And leather skin
Will sour milk
And curdle blood.
They give your house
The creeping crud
That kills the plants.
To tease the pets,
They round them up
In ragged nets.
You fall asleep,
They interfere
By pouring night-
mares in your ear.
They steal children
Where they may—
It's part of nasty
Goblin play!
If you don't own
A rolling pin—
Don't *ever* let
The Goblins in.

October Talk

Says the cornstalk
Ears
can hear
whispertalk

Say the shadows
Leap
surprise

Sighs the night wind
Wish I wish

Says a mother
to a witchy girl
Ride

Says my cat
black on the new moon
Oh

Shouts the house on the hill
Come round
all around

Sings the barn owl
Home

Incident on Beggar's Night

Griselda Grump
  Wore ragged clothes,
  A pointy hat,
  A putty nose,
    And when she found
    The kitchen broom,
    She sailed around
    The living room.
    She said, "I'm not
    About to quit
    Until I've got
    The hang of it!"
  At first she kept
Her eyes shut tight
Until she swept
Into the night. . . .
  Grump softly bumped
  Against a cloud!
    She cackled, thumped
    It, cried out loud:
    "Oh, look at what
    A world I see.
    **I THINK I'VE GOT
    THE HANG OF ME!"**
  Griselda steered
Up, up and soon,
She disappeared
Behind the moon.

Hoppy Zappitello

The new sub, Mr. Orr,
tells us the math test
has 50 hard questions.
"To receive an A, you
have to get 90 percent right,"
he says. *Great*, I'm
thinking, *that's a mind
bender all by itself.*
Then Hoppy "the Brain"
Zappitello leans over
and says to me, "Just for
fun, I think I'll get 111 percent
of the 90 percent right. So how
many will I knock out
of the park, Einstein?"
My name, in case you
were wondering, is not
Einstein. It's Weinstein . . .
with a W! So what's
the answer I should tell
the Brain (before I say,
"Stick a sock in it, Hoppy!")?

ANSWER: Hoppy will get all 50 questions correct.
$90 \times 50 = 45$; $1.11 \times 45 = 49.95$,
which, rounded up, equals 50.

The Loneliest Creature

"Lonesome George"
Giant tortoise, the only survivor on
Abingdon Island, Ecuador

I cannot talk but to the wind,
I cannot play the old shell game.
I cannot see far out to sea.
I heard a voice, but no one came.

What fate awaits a ragged king
Beyond that dune, a rugged climb?
The seasons change too late, too soon;
I have too much, too little time.

Epitaphs

For a Doctor

Took two aspirins—had a cough.
Went to bed—pajamas off.

Died, which turned out for the best—
Didn't have to get undressed.

For a Jockey

Everybody felt remorse,
Except the horse.

For a Plastic Surgeon

He took in hips,
He tucked in chins,
He fattened lips,
And smoothed out skins,
Unwrinkled eyes,
And narrowed noses.
Now here he lies...

And decomposes.

Bad Pretzels

A pretzel baked without a twist
Is like the knuckleball you missed.
A pretzel made without a weave
Is only pretzel make-believe.
The pretzels that are never bent
Taste like, say, 25 percent
Of pretzels twisted like an 8.
Oh, never eat your pretzels straight.

American Autumn

O
H,
O
A
K
T
R
E
E,
Y
O
U
L
E
F
T
SUCH
A HEAP!
THE FRONT-
YARD LEAVES
ARE GETTING DEEP
AND I HAVE PREMISES
TO KEEP AND PILES TO
GO THAT I MUST SWEEP AND
PILES TO GO THAT I MUST SWEEP

For a Teacher Gone Too Soon

You're not here.
Those three small words shroud the year
like drifting snow. Our classroom,
tomb
of your laughter,
whispers its gratitude after
the gift we never outgrew . . .
you.

128 Uneasy Ed

An excitable bird was Uneasy Ed Kohler,
Who fancied himself a 300-game bowler.
His team (thanks to Ed, way ahead in the scoring)
Wore shirts that read, "$Cleveland Linoleum Flooring$."

The crowd had gone quiet—Uneasy was ready—
But down on lane 7, somebody yelled, "Eddie!"
He lofted the ball! You could hear the boards shudder!

It crept down the lane and rolled into the

G
U
T
T
E
R
!

How Fast Do They Go?

27.89 mph for a human being

(fleeing)

.03 mph for a garden snail

(trail)

32 mph for a white-tailed deer

(fear)

68 mph for the fastest fish

(splish)

2,193 mph for the fastest jet

(yet)

45.98 mph for the fastest sub

(glub!)

51.1 mph for the fastest tank

(clank)

4.8 feet per hour for the fastest-moving glacier

(erasure)

15 inches per second for the fastest caterpillar

(thriller!)

105 mph for the fastest motorcycle handlebar wheelie

(really?)

Revenge

From your great elm tree, late night winds'll

```
    F       F       F
  L       L       L
  U       U       U
  T       T       T
      E       E       E
      R       R       R


      T       T       T
      O       O       O
      I       I       I
  L       L       L
  E       E       E
  T       T       T


      P       P       P
      A       A       A
  P       P       P
      E       E       E
      R       R       R

  T       T       T
  I       I       I
    N       N       N
    S       S       S
  E       E       E
      L       L       L
```

The Bottomless Well

What do you see when you look down a well
But blackness? Does the deep undock your mind?
And do you feel the tingling magic spell?
Or wonder what the silence leaves behind?
They say a boy, Elijah Willingham,
The butcher's son who disappeared last fall,
Was playing in the neighborhood with Sam
O'Shaughnessy, and bounced a basketball
Into the village Well of Endlessness.
Now it was dark and Sam went home to bed.
The ball? Elijah thought he could finesse
It from the watery grave where it had fled.
The endless possibilities have drowned.
No ball or butcher boy was ever found.

Doctor, Doctor, Sick in Bed

Doctor, Doctor, sick in bed,
Called the vet. And the vet doc said,
"Doctor, take a few weeks off—
It cured my cow of the whooping cough.
If that won't work, then take these pills—
It cured my horse of the bloomin' chills.
If that won't work, I'll give you a shot—
It cured my pig of the spindle-rot.
If that won't work, I'll saw off your leg—
It cured my neighbor's sister, Peg.
And if *that* won't work," the vet doc cried,
"Doctor, Doctor, you done died!"

123 Limb-ericks: Hip Verses

The Neck

According to *Good Gnus Reporter*,
The Giraffe used to be a lot shorter
   Till a bird in the trees
   Said, "Get up off your knees!"
Said Giraffe, "That's a very tall order."

The Arm

To an Octopus luncheon for nine,
The comrades-in-arms come to dine.
   But when hugging each other—
   What suckers, oh brother!—
They look like a great ball of twine.

The Antler

The Moose suffers pain and distress
If a hat is hung on his headdress.
   His horns were intended
   For something more splendid—
But what it is no one can guess!

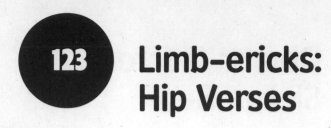

Dad Tells Me

It's bad enough when you forget,
But even worse if you forgot
That you forgot something, and yet
You can't be sure exactly what.

If I had a forget-me-not,
Then I Forgot Day I would know
But I forget what I forgot—
It came and went . . . three days ago!

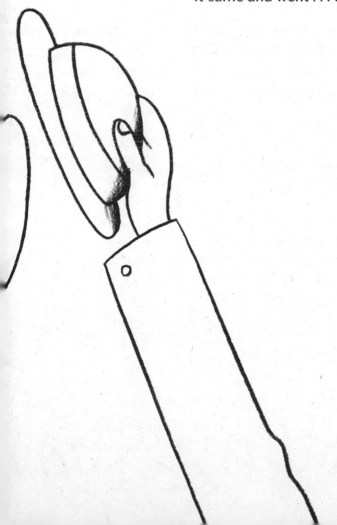

Barnabas Bear & Victoria Pig

When Barnabas Bear began losing his hair,
He tried every cure that he could—
From vinegar lotions to mayonnaise potions,
But none of them did any good.

He went for advice, two pennies the price,
To a Mrs. Victoria Pig,
A teller of fortune, who sat on her porch in
A beautiful piggledy-wig.

Victoria said as she looked at his head—
She knew she was being quite careless—
"Don't think me too bold, but have you been told,
You're un*bear*ably handsome hairless?"

Barnabas blushed and suddenly crushed
The toadstool under his rear.
And from that day on, though his hair was long gone,
He knew he had nothing to fear.

They invite him to teas and to spelling bees—
Oh, nothing you'd think of as formal.
And after they greet him, they actually treat him
As if he was perfectly normal.

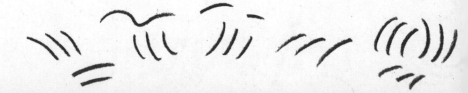

120 Midnot Hoku

Listen . . . on the hill
a hoot owl is *chwoooing* one
syllable of wind

Mr. Must-Have-Forgot

There was a young man,
Mr. Must-Have-Forgot,
Who couldn't remember
"What for?" and "Why not?"
Everyday questions,
Like "How do you do?"
Completely escaped him—
He hadn't a clue.

One morning a lady
Made bold to exclaim,
"I'm Alice. Pray tell me, sir,
What is your name?"
The cat got his tongue
And tied it in a knot,
"N-name? Why, of course!
Mr. Must Have—"

Thanksgiving Dinner, Anywhere, U.S.A.

Behind the milk
glass bowl,
a farmer ant

has set beside
a drop of water
from a plant

three crumbs
of new brown
bread.

Before the feast
begins, she
bows her head.

The Menu at the First Thanksgiving, 1621

The Pilgrims likely brought no pigs across:
That first Thanksgiving they would eat no ham,
No mashed potato, sweet potato, yam,
For lack of sugar, no cranberry sauce.
Corn on the cob would not have been around.
A pumpkin pie? Not even in their dreams.
And yet the bounty was a match, it seems,
For this historic day on hallowed ground.
Wild turkey, goose, duck, swan, partridge, and crane,
Cod, bass, herring, bluefish, and eels released
Uncommon bonds of gratitude. That feast
Would be their last. They never met again—
The Indians and Pilgrims—to break bread.
But that Thanksgiving Day they were well-fed.

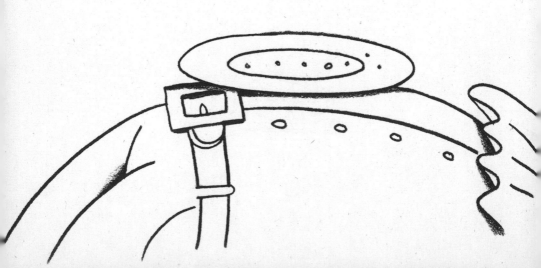

116 Library Fine

OVERDUE's the dreaded word
I *never* want to hear,
Especially if it's followed
By two other words—

A YEAR!

A Football Poem

A football poem
Should hit hard
Like a nose guard,

Or spiral through the sky
Like a down-and-out pass
On *real* grass.

A football poem
Should score
Inside the five
On fourth and four.

A football poem
Should sweat, talk trash, and grunt . . .
Or punt.

Girl and Boy

She liked this kid, but she didn't like me.
"Oh, well," I said, "other fish in the sea."

She said, "Even though I don't like you,
There are plenty of other apes in the zoo."

I said, "Okay, I'll find another fish."
So I went to the sea, and I got my wish.

She went to the zoo for a guy like me,
And now she likes this chimpanzee.

Small Talk in the Neighborhood

I said, "Hello, how do you do?"
He said, "Oh, pretty good, and you?"

He said, "Well, how about this rain?"
I said, "The weather's been a pain."

I said, "And when it rains, it pours."
He said, "We'll have to get the oars."

There wasn't any more to say—
We said the same thing yesterday.

Loosey Qwill

Loosey Qwill and I are birds,
Feeding on the choicest words:
She the parrot, I the bard
At 1 Library Boulevard.

Loosey chatters to her small
Audience—the kitchen wall.
My voice rings! Who overhears?
None but half a dozen ears.

She is anxious in her cage.
I would like a larger stage,
But how wonderful to have
Our vocabulary salve.

While she practices her s's
For her Gettysbird addresses,
Lucky me if, once a day,
I can find one thing to say.

So to manufacture words
Like so many poet birds,
We plant posies round the room,
Egging, begging them to bloom.

Endlessly we seek to fly
(Sitting still but) far away,
Loosey Qwill, my bird, and I,
Birds at work with words at play.

111 Conc-luge-ion

Cried a spunky young lady from Bruges,
"Oh, what fun to be racing the luge!"
    But the sled overshot—
    The young lady did not—
And it left her behind rather rouge.

Lloyd Q. Boyd, Goalie Humanoid

Now here's a tale you may have heard
About a first-class fifth-grade nerd,
Who, once he wore a chest protector,
A face (of **Frankenstein!**) deflector,
Ice skates, jersey, pads and mitts,
Gave all opposing teams the fits.
They shoved him around like a tiddly-wink . . .
Until he rumbled on the rink!
The ice would groan and creak and crunch,
While he ate hockey pucks for lunch.
And no one messed with Lloyd Q. Boyd,
The fifth-grade Ice Age humanoid.

Animal Epitaphs

FOR A SHEEP
NO ONE WILL EVER FORGET EWE

FOR A BOLL WEEVIL
GONE BUT NOT FOR COTTON

FOR A SKUNK
HE WON'T BE MIST

FOR A PIGEON
SHE WAS POOPED

FOR A FIREFLY
SHE WAS NOT THE SUN
SHE WAS NOT THE STARS
BUT SHE WAS LOTS OF FUN
IN MAYONNAISE JARS

FOR A MOTH
IN CASE I COME BACK,
LEAVE THE PORCH LIGHT ON

FOR A MOUSE
Miss the traps
Miss the cheese
Miss the cheddars
Miss the bries
Miss the Colbys
Miss the Swisses
Miss the Muensters
Miss the Mrs.

Food Fight

There's one big holiday whose date
I wish we wouldn't celebrate.
It's when the in-laws come to dine—
Linebackers in a buffet line.
And when they all sit down to chow,
Think of a pig trough—*Holy Cow!*
When you hear spaghetti slurps,
Choruses of meatball burps,
Cousin Rayford licks the bowl
Of the three-bean casserole.
Uncle Lester shoots, "unseen,"
At his wife a lima bean.
Auntie Olive (maniac)
Spears a bun and fires back.
When it bounces off the twins,
That's when Whirl War III begins.
Laughing crazies pitch their food—
Normal people come unglued.
Half a minute's what it takes
To look like melting wedding cakes.
Dad grins in his gooey shirt,
"Anybody want dessert?"

The School Principal

The principal at the school I attend
Is someone every kid has come to know
As Doctor L.; the *L* stands for LaFoe—
Jill Martin thinks it ought to be LaFriend.
She tousles Brandon's hair, then bumps a fist
With Leroy Long, pretending she's a jock.
She spins and beats the buzzer on the clock.
It doesn't really matter that she missed.
So what if Dr. L. goes overboard.
The students know she plays a different game,
But hers and theirs are pretty much the same:
A measure of respect is her reward.
All I know is that when you see her grin,
You almost want the school day to begin.

First Kwanzaa*

Zawadi—simple gifts,
Vibunzi—ears of corn,
Mishumaa saba—candles
Where ancestors were born.

Mkeka—straw place mat,
For food from many lands,
Mazao—fruit and vegetables
Prepared by many hands.

The feast begins in praise.
Rejoicing, lifting up
Their lives, they drink to life
From this communal cup.

The bountiful year ends,
With breaking of the bread,
The fellowship of friends,
The year of hope ahead.

*Kwanzaa, meaning "first fruits," is an African-American festival on December 26–January 1. It was first celebrated in 1966.

105 Hanukkah Lights

Verse: Let the miracle and aura
Of eight lights from that menorah
Lit from one small vial of oil
Call the faithful from their toil.

Chorus: As each house begins its glowing,
People coming, people going
Mark a time—the overthrowing,
The defeat of the invaders.
People born in every nation
Celebrate our liberation.

Verses: Let us keep the promise simple:
To rededicate the Temple
With a symbol to inspire
Peace and Freedom—candlefire.

Let no enemies destroy us
In a season turning joyous,
For it's Hanukkah that's bringing
Children laughing, children singing.

But let every child remember
That this festival in December,
So enriching a revival,
Is a hymn to our survival.

Chorus: As each house begins its glowing,
People coming, people going
Mark a time—the overthrowing,
The defeat of the invaders.
People born in every nation
Celebrate our liberation.

104 North Polar Pie

In Santa's toy factory, two elves
Are inspecting the deep-freezer shelves
  When what catches their eye
  But a North Polar Pie
They decide they should taste for themselves.

In a blender goes marshmallow fluff,
Chocolate syrup, and more gooey stuff,
  And one elf bellows, "Brenda,
  Your sweet tooth! The Splenda—
Two tablespoons should be enough."

Now they wait till the Polar Pie thaws—
Oh, the damage it does to your jaws!—
  Then the elves put the Pie
  In the blender on HIGH,
And they slurp it through curlicue straws.

Dreidl Rhyme

Dreidl, dreidl, what's to eat?
Show me something *very* sweet!

Put one candy in the middle,
Spin the dreidl just a little—

If the dreidl comes up *shin* שׁ
Put one piece of candy in.

If it's half—the letter *hey* ה —
Take half of the pot away.

If the *gimel* ג should appear,
You win everything, my dear!

But if *nun* נ should show its face,
Someone else spins in your place.

Now before we spin again,
Put another candy in.

Dreidl, dreidl, what's to eat?
Show me something *very* sweet!

102 Hurry Hound

I remember long ago,
When rooftops tipped with drifted snow,
The hound of all my winters who
Hurried home the winters through.
Have you seen my hurry hound
Leaping fast, a furry sound?
Have you smoothed her winter mane
Turning burning gold again?

Did you see how high she flew
One evening when the moon was new,
Chasing the Dog Star deep in space,
Twitching in dreams by the fireplace,
Lapping water, begging a bone,
Making half my bed her own,
Waltzing the cat with fumble paws,
Jumping up on Santa Claus . . . ?

I remember long ago,
When rooftops tipped with drifted snow,
The hound of all my winters who
Hurried home the winters through.
And I remember even now
The violin of the cat's meow
On those iced nights when she would come
     . . . and the quiet pandemonium.

101 Oh Calendar!

To see
December press
Its face against the door,
I realize I've grown an inch
Or more

Since we
First hung you up.
You measured time by turns,
Hard winter nights to softball days,
Sunburns,

The chill
At Halloween,
Then, rumors of reindeer
Across the sky. Good-bye, Happy
Old Year!

Watching the New Year's Eve Party Through the Staircase

100

Now midnight's here,
    The year is gone;
The merrymakers
    Carry on.

Instead of hats,
    They've sprouted horns
That make them look
    Like unicorns.

Tin whizzers buzz,
    Click-clackers clap,
Confetti snows
    Down Mrs. Knapp.

My mother's fruitcakes
    Disappear.
The dancers shake
    The chandelier,

The floor, the windows . . . !
    Maybe this
Is why they stop
    Sometimes and kiss.

New Year Letter of Good Cheer

The  has turned the year, and the occasion

Deserves a celebration. Can't you feel it?

I'll ✂ a sheet of ▱ into pieces,

Then stick them in an ✉ , and 🦭 it.

And send it to my friends—Leigh Ann and Matty,

Beth, Melissa, Kelly, Scott and Eddie—

To 👓, my 🦌 , that what they celebrate with

Are 2 enormous 🖐 fuls of confetti!

First of Jan. Hey, snowman!	First of Feb. Old spiderweb	Middle of Mar. Spring can't be far
First of Ap. Soggy landscape	First of May Petunia day!	First of June Can't come too soon
Fourth of Jul. Swimming pool!	First of Aug. Croaking frog	First of Sept. Overslept!
Last of Oct. *Someone knocked!*	First of Nov. Light the stove	End of Dec. Dove of peace

97 Two Snowflakes

Said Crystal Snowflake to her twin,
  "Look at what a spin I'm in
  Circling over Buffalo!"

  Said her sister Ivory, "Oh,
    Let us snow then, you and I,
    While we have dry winds to fly."

    Crystal cried, "In paradise
    We'd continue life as ice.
    Or perhaps we could exist
    Momentarily as mist?"

      Ivory scolded Crystal, "Hush!
      We just might wind up as slush."

      Happily they wound up stuck
      To a refrigerated truck!

96 Band-Aid

Rosebud of blood
  Bubbles and smears.
I brush the mud
  And dry my tears,

Thankful I have
  That peace of tape
From Mom or Dad
  For cut and scrape.

Out of the blue,
  A first-aid kit
Turns "Ouch" to "Oooh,"
  And in a bit

This three-inch patch
  Will let me play
Because the scratch
  Is "stripped" away.

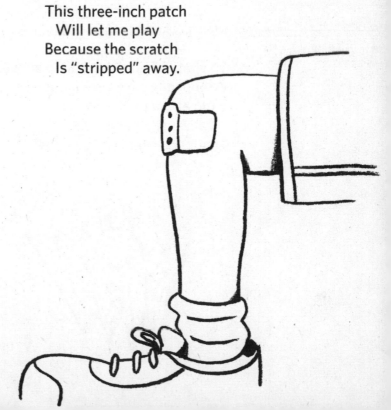

Limb-ericks: Hip Verses

The Skin

Now a snake who's about to begin
Climbing out of his ugly old skin
　　Has the grin of a winner—
　　It's "in" to be inner
And out of the outer he's in.

The Hump

In the desert a camel was minus
A passenger, His Royal Highness.
　　The King loved the humps
　　But the bumpety-bumps
Left him down in the dumps and the dryness.

The Nose

The bat clings to the ceiling above,
Wrapped in wings like a hand in a glove,
　　Too afraid to expose
　　To his neighbors a nose
That only a mother could love.

94 Lives of Distance Runners

Lives of distance runners tell us
Victory goes to the young,
Exuberant, and overzealous
Kid who has an extra lung.

I'm Off to New London

I'm off to New London
To buy a good husband
To put in the kitchen
When company comes.
He'll nod when he's told to
And nod when he's old, too.
"How clever!" they'll say,
As he twiddles his thumbs.

The Cows in France

The Cows in France

In Paris, France the cows say *meuuuu*
Because they know the *parlez-vous*.

But they have nothing much to say
To horses speaking English—*neigh*,

The cows who *cheu* their *qud* and *meuuuu*
In fancy Frenchy *parlez-vous*.

The Chess Battle

Knight said to the Queen, "My Lady Fair,
Please take a seat on Your Majesty's square.
I've sounded the trumpets, assembled the Pawns.
     We haven't a minute to spare!"

Bishop said to the King, "Your castle, my lord,
Is safe from attack. Squire Rook is on board."
"My Square Table Knights," His Highness replied,
     "Can advance without drawing a sword!"

But the White Knights were captured,
The Pawns scooped away,
     And the Rooks went to sleep in the corner.
When the King fell to pieces,
The Queen stood alone
     For the Bishops had failed to warn her!

She wanted to scream at them,
"Look what you've done!"
     But how could it do any good?
The Rooks and the Bishops
Had heads made of marble;
     The Pawns were all carved out of wood.

Papa Bear

Papa is a morning bear—
Showers, pats his grizzly hair,
Throws his clothes on, scares the cat,
Shuffles down to breakfast. That
Closet is his hiding place—

Boo!—hugs Mama, rubs my face
With his whiskers, eats his grits,
Likes to growl before he sIts
In his den to read the news,
Winks at me, unties his shoes;
Papa's ready for a snooze.

New York
Public Library

The Wild Words roar
In the Lion House.
When you come

For a visit, they
Reach out and grab you
And shake you.

They won't let you go
Without taking a few
Of them home.

You needn't worry;
They won't bite.
The Wild Words that live

In the Lion House
Love to feed
The customers.

Polar Bear Rap

Weather be chilly,
Weather be nice
Whether we swimmin'
Up over de ice.

Whether we eatin'
Paw-lickin' sweet
Saturday, Sunday,
Monday meat.

Weather be sleetin',
Weather be snow
Whether we stayin'
But we gotta go.

Weather be nuttin'
Less'n me 'n' you
Bust on outta this
Nuttin' much zoo.

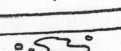

Martin Luther King, Jr. Day

Imagine
How
A single
Voice
Echoes
Across
Decades
Repeating
Equality
And justice
Matter

Nicholas Needham

Book Head Case and Bookcase Head

You can read him like a book
Nicholas Needham — take a look:
As he   grew a book-   case head
(For he   readandread   and read)
He would need 'em through the years
Bookmark nose   and bookend ears
Grew enormous   bookworm eyes
Nicholas Need-   ham, child-size,
Barely three feet from the floor
Sprouted up and read some more
Lucky, as a   little weed,
Nicholas Needham   learned to read

85 I Like a Day

I like a sun
As breakfast has begun

I like a rain
On rooftops to complain

I like a snow
Unsure which way to blow

I like a fog
That bedspread of a bog

I like a hail
The clouds' express airmail

I like a storm
That promises no harm

I like a wind
To leave clotheslines unpinned

I like midnight
To *wet* its appetite

I like a dawn
Because it turns day on

I like a day
When weather's out to play

A Rhyme for Orange

The King commanded twelve wise men
To find a rhyme for "orange."
And while they thought
And thought some more,
There came a squeaking at the door.
The King cried, *"Fix that door 'inge!"*

The SS
Hot Dog Bun

To take the most delicious trip
Across the mackerel-crowded sea
Requires a tasty little ship
To get you where you want to be.

Oh, there's a catsup-colored stripe
Across a mustard-colored boat
That has an onion steering wheel
And pickle decks. It stays afloat
By steaming in the frying sun.
It's called the SS *Hot Dog Bun!*

Though it is but a dinghy thing
To everyone onboard the cruise,
The *Hot Dog*'s cook is offering
Any delicacy you chews.

Rabbit Math

Two rabbits near Grand Central Station
Were creating a mild sensation.
    They could add and subtract—
    And no hiding the fact—
They were whizzes at multiplication!

Quatrains on the Weather

A hurricane is what you see
When winds in coats of cruelty
Tear them off and whip them round
A barn and rip it off the ground.

* *

What is the rain if not a sky
So frightened that it starts to cry?
What is the hail if not a cloud
That's playing street drums *very* loud?

* *

Our world is white-on-white tonight.
The sleet that's falling isn't quite
As white as that first snow that fell
In swirls riding a carousel.

* *

One day the sun thought that it would
Be fun to skip our neighborhood.
It stopped to glare three blocks away
At children who came out to play.

Punxsutawney Phil

There's a smallish, fur footballish
Animal whose name is Phil.
He's from Punxsutawney, PA,
And he knows the yearly drill.
You reach inside his hole and feel around
Then pull him out—
This weatherman who knows beyond
The shadow of a doubt
How to make you feel springtime fresh
Or else keep up the cold.
Will spring come early? Six weeks more
Of winter uncontrolled?
To Phil it doesn't matter what
He sees outside his mound—
Phil will get his fill of sleeping
Snugly underground.

Mr. Mack Celebrates the 100th Day of School

Assignment, students, write a story—
"Tomorrow is the Hundredth Day"—
And tell me what's so hunky-dory
About it in a funky way.

You might begin with "Listen, homey,
Tomorrow is the hundredth day
With wacky Mr. Mack." You know me.
What would you really like to say

About your favorite English teacher?
Tomorrow is the hundredth day.
Describe my most amazing feature.
And no, I don't wear a toupee!

Good-bye to an Architect

The alligator, who perverse-
ly pinned his prey, is now a purse.

The riddle of the Sphinx, I'd say,
Is how his nose got blown away.

The cow, once so self-satisfied,
Is furniture in Naugahyde.

Great dinosaurs patrol museums
To contemplate their mausoleums.

And I, who built factories and plants,
Am fertilizing farms for ants!

The Dragon Dance

A Chinese New Year cannot fade
From memory if it goes on
With one great Dragon Dance parade—

The highlight of the cavalcade.
If you've seen this phenomenon,
A Chinese New Year cannot fade.

From silk, paper, bamboo is made
A symbol to enlarge upon
In one great Dragon Dance parade.

The dragon sits on poles conveyed
By men who swirl a marathon:
A Chinese New Year cannot fade.

Chinese believe they have displayed
Their forebear from prehistory's dawn
In one great Dragon Dance parade.

A world so brilliantly arrayed
From Beijing to Saskatchewan,
The Chinese New Year cannot fade
With that great Dragon Dance parade.

The Ninth Ward
Hurricane Katrina
New Orleans

Earlene Boudreau did not expect to die
The day the levees broke, but oh my Lord,
Her miracle went to a passerby.

She heard the crackling bullhorn notify
Them help was on its way to the Ninth Ward.
Earlene Boudreau did not expect to die.

A helicopter did not hear the cry,
A girl strapped to a chimney by a cord.
Her miracle flew to a passerby.

The water rose as much as nine feet high.
A flatboat came; she could not climb aboard.
Earlene Boudreau did not expect to die.

The government stuck to its alibi:
High cost of safety it could ill afford.
Her miracle went to a passerby.

The headline news: "A Nation Wonders Why
Katrina's Homeless Victims Are Ignored."
Earlene Boudreau did not expect to die:
Her miracle went to a passerby.

75 The Brains

The Queen of Brains
Often complains,
She says the King has none;
The Prince of Brains
Says, "What remains
Of brains—there's hardly one!"

The King of Brains
Stands out in rains—
The poor man knows no better,
Because a royal
Brain contains
Cottage cheese and cheddar.

No, Bull!

Ever try to pet a bull?
The feeling's unforgettable,
That beast is so incredible.
   Don't ever try to pet him.

To estimate the loss a bull
Can cause is quite impossible.
A bull is so unbossible—
   You'd better not upset him.

Far off he looks adorable,
But my advice? Ignore a bull.
Up close he's truly horrible.
   If you could just confuse him . . .

But boy oh boy oh boy, a bull
Would find it most enjoyable
To leave you unemployable.
   You've got two legs, so use 'em!

73 The Toilet Inspector

Here at the Ritz Ambassador,
I am the 87th floor
    Toilet Inspection Man.
I see to it with bristle brush
That drains unclog and toilets flush—
    Or else I kick the can.

I man the bucket and the mop.
The elevator will not stop
    At 87 when
The LADIES overflows, the GENTS
Backs up, and then in self-defense
    It overflows again.

They pay me just to be relieved
Of odors not to be believed—
    Excuse my saying so,
But management will not abide
A toilet seat whose underside
    Smells like a rodeo.

Marshmallow, Banana, Dill Pickle

There is something about a marshmallow,
So soft, irresistibly gooey,
Fluffy stuff of a puffy marshmallow,
Just enough and deliciously chewy.
There is something about a marshmallow
The marshmallow is trying to hide;
And it isn't the powder
Surrounding the outer
White skin, it's the secret inside.

There is something about a banana
That we serve as a curvy hors d'oeuvre.
What a beautiful fruit, a banana!
But pay close attention, observe:
There is something about a banana—
One way to describe it is icky:
On the sides of the thing
Is the long yellow string
That is most unappeelingly sticky!

There is something about a dill pickle
That no other pickle can claim.
You really can't say it's a tickle
Or pinch though it's nearly the same.
There is something about a dill pickle
That everyone knows as a pucker
And a pickle like this
Makes a vinegar kiss
That could even bring tears to a trucker!

Miss Treat

I loved you when I wrote this line
because you were my Valentine.
But you turned out to be so mean!
Now you are my Halloween!

Valentine's Day At Sea

February 14
Captain's Log
The Frisky Dog

Up through the fog came *The Frisky Dog*
    With me and my forty-man crew.
We were tightly packed, as a matter of fact,
    For *The Dog* is a bark canoe.

Now the pop-eyed cook took a pop-eyed look,
    And he saw what we came to see:
The courtship swoon by a midnight moon
    Of an Octopus he and she.

They kissed on the lips and the slithery hips,
    They kissed on the suction cups.
And they bobbed in the brine like a ball of twine
    Till at last the bosun ups,

And he shouts, "I'm Dutch, but I never saw such
    Sweet love on Valentine's Day!"
Then arm in arm . . . in arm . . . in arm . . . ,
    The Octopi bobbed away.

69 **Riddle**

What starts
with D,
ends with D,
has a D
in the middle,
and makes
you turn
your car
around?

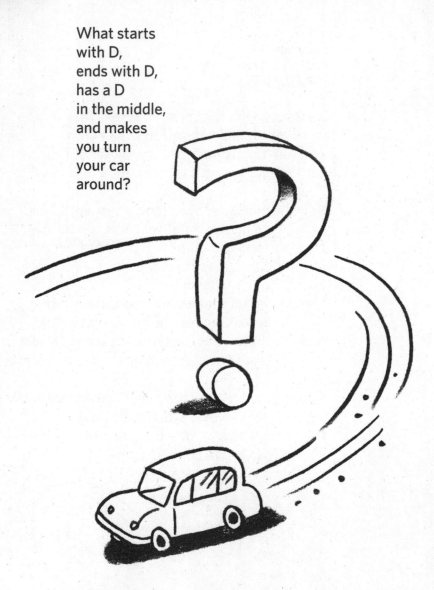

ANSWER: Dead end

68 The School Custodian

I've seen them come and go for forty years—
The jocks, the brains, the show-offs and the shy.
They hang around my room, I can't say why.
It could be that I represent their fears
And frailties so vulnerable to harm.
They ask me things, like *Tell us, Mr. V.,*
About the time you were a refugee.
Where did you get the numbers on your arm?
And I describe it all—or some of it.
The curiosity of easy youth
Is trumped by innocence. For them, the truth
Attends to what is often counterfeit.
And then there is the ringing of the bell:
They've heard about as much as I can tell.

Syllables

Words of one syllable **sigh,**
Words of two syllables **reply,**
Words of three syllables **clarify,**
Words of four syllables **intensify,**
Words of five syllables **overspecify,**
Words of six . . . **why?**

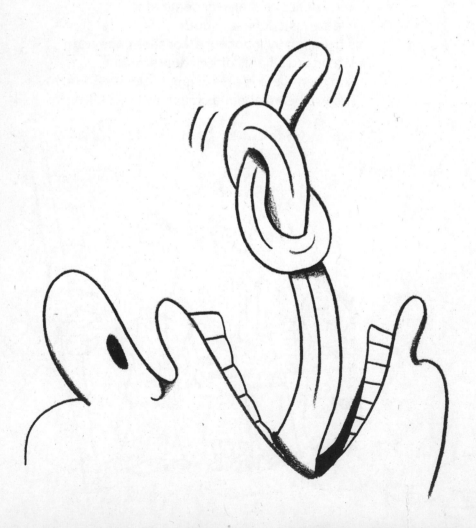

The Hippopotabus
(A Book-Boat)

A bookmobile, extremely large,
A floating minibus
That travels like a steaming barge
Of hippopotamus,

Holds fables, facts, tiptoe tall tales,
Bookshelves of derring-do,
And poetry that never fails
To hippnotize the crew.

Turn any page. First port of call
On RIVER LONGAGO!
"We've reached," says Book-Boat's Admiral,
"The town of MAYBESO,

"Whose lovely tribe, the BRARIANS,
Keepers of verbs and nouns,
Will introduce you to WORDGRRRS,
The literary hounds.

"So this trip promises to be
Wordplayfularious,
A bonbon bon voyage to sea
By Hippopotabus!"

65 Skunk

It's not enough
She makes us
Spray our clothes,
She also makes us
Pay through the nose.

64 Civil War Couplets

What is the highest price of freedom?
Bull Run, Gettysburg, Antietam.

* *

Up North, three hundred dollars could recruit
A soldier who would be your substitute.

* *

Blue Generals: Grant, McClellan, Hancock, Hooker, Blair
Gray Generals: Lee, Magruder, Pickett, Hood, Despair

* *

If six hundred twenty thousand soldiers lost their lives,
How many mothers, fathers, daughters, sons, and wives?

* *

An actor by the name of John Wilkes Booth
Assassinated Hope and murdered Truth.

He Heard the Owl

Considering that Half the Day
 Had trotted into Night,
The baker's boy fell up to sleep—
 His eyes were open tight.
And he awoke so hungry that
 He'd lost his appetite.

He heard the Owl upon the hill
 Vow vowels to the Moon.
"How doo you doo?" Owl said. "Would you
 Be my true blue balloon?"
Across the sky came Moon's reply—
 "I'll meet you here at noon."

Sir Wind strolled in with Teapot Rain
 As if they'd met before.
He swept her off her feet, and then
 Sir Wind began to roar.
The baker's boy replied, "You'll only
 Make Miss Teapot pour!"

And so she did, and oh she did!—
 Torrential waterspout.
Likewise the lonely Owl wept
 To let his feelings out,
For when Moon fled, she did not shed
 The shadow of a doubt.

No Matter Where You Go

Isn't it awfully
nice to know
that no matter
where you go,
Timbuktu or Tokyo,
Montreal, New York,
or Rome,
people there
still call it . . ."Home"?

*Focolare, hus, das Haus,
hogar, talo, spiti, haz,
lakas, etxe, casa, dom.*

There's always room
at home for "Home."

The Dancing Black Bear

There once was a dancing black bear,
Who, instead of a hat, wore a pair
    Of boots on his head.
     "It's the two-step," he said,
"And it feels like I'm walking on air!"

60 Tweedle Dumb and Tweedle Smart

Tweedle Dumb and Tweedle Smart
Decided they would travel.
They rode around in a shopping cart
On cinnamon and gravel.

They met the King and Queen for tea!
Said Tweedleboy, the Smarter,
Ah me, to be like royalty
We should have studied harder.

When Is Its It's?

"Its" is a possessive.
"It's" is not.
"It's" is "It is,"
As in "It is *what?*"

Here's the reason why:
That apostrophe
In "It's" stands for "i"—
That's where an "i" should be.

It's easy to confuse
"Its" with "It's."
So always remember
Which "Its" it's that fits.

58 Who Can Tell?

Poor is poor
And rich is rich,
But in the bathtub,
Which is which?

Country Haik-lues

White Nights to Red Square
people love their potatoes—
and onion churches

Russia

* *

You know me by my
nation's symbols—maple leaf
and mounted police

Canada

* *

Chocolate capital
famous for its St. Bernards
higher than a kite

Switzerland

* *

African hot spot
for great wildlife safaris—
wildebeest haven

Kenya

* *

Where everybody
wears a caste, curries favor,
and favors curry

India

56 Bigfoot

DESCRIPTION:

Shape:
Ape.
Furry,
Blurry,
In a hurry;
Hairy,
Scary,
Legendary
Nature streaker.
Biggest ever
Nike sneaker.
Last seen?
Halloween!
If he's found,
Turn around.
If he's mad,
Egad!
If he's close,
Ewwww, gross!
Hear the crunch?
You're lunch.

55 Alphabet Game

Mickey played golf and T'd the ball.
Matty played pool and Q'd the ball.
Andy played catch and I'd the ball.
Timmy played a baby and P'd is all.

54 The Reason for Rainbows
An Ode to Baseball

There was an Old Man of Late Summer
Met a Winter Boy out of the blue,
And he whisked him away
From the city one day
Just to show him what country boys do.

He taught him three whys of a rooster,
And he showed him two hows of a hen.
Then he'd try to bewitch him
With curveballs he'd pitch him
Again and again and again.

He taught him the reason for rainbows,
And he showed him why lightning was king,
Then he fingered the last ball—
A wicked hop fastball—
He threw to the plate on a string.

[Chorus]

Oh, the Old Summer Man and the Young Winter Lad
Spent the light of each day—every moment they had—
In the wind and the rain, or the late summer sun,
Where he taught him to pitch and he taught him to run
In the wind and rain and the late summer sun.

But when that Old Man of Late Summer
Met the Winter Boy out of the blue,
He said to him, "Son,
You can pitch, you can run,
But to hit here is what you must do:

"Just pretend that the stick on your shoulder
Is as wide as a bald eagle's wing.
You're a bird on a wire
And your hands are on fire—
But you're never too eager to swing.

"Stand as still as a rabbit in danger,
Watch the pitch with the eyes of a cat.
What will fly past the mound—
Unforgettable sound—
Is the ball as it cracks off the bat."

Oh, the Old Summer Man and the Young Winter Lad
Spent the light of each day—every moment they had—
In the wind and the rain, or the late summer sun,
Where he taught him to pitch and he taught him to run
In the wind and rain and the late summer sun.

53 The Birthday Cake Song

1. When I was a boy
   On a pretty Great Lake,
   We called it heaven
   Watching Grandma bake
   Butternut batter
   Into birthday cake—
   Sprinkles and icing,
   Goodness' sake!
   First slice Timmy,
   Second slice Mick,
   Third slice Dickey
   Disappeared right quick.
   Fourth slice Harry,
   Fifth slice Buzz.
   Who was the last cake-boy?
   I was!

2. When Granny got a gander
   At the birthday food,
   She tied on her apron
   In a holiday mood.
   She beat pure vanilla
   Into butter once more—
   In went the batter
   We were waiting for!
   First slice Timmy,
   Second slice Mick,
   Third slice Dickey
   Disappeared right quick.
   Fourth slice Harry,
   Fifth slice Buzz.
   Who was the last cake-boy?
   I was!

3. Two buttercakes gone
   And we all felt sick.
   Granny got madder
   Than a hound-dog tick.
   Into the oven popped
   One more treat—
   Out popped a buttercake—
   Granny said, *"EAT!"*
   First slice Timmy,
   Second slice Mick,
   Third slice Dickey
   Disappeared right quick.
   Fourth slice Harry,
   Fifth slice Buzz.
   Who was the last cake-boy?
   I was!

Riddle

Here's a six-letter word
That's a pet like mine.
If you take away 2,
You will still have 9!

ANSWER: ǝuᴉuɐɔ

Doozies for Twosies: Animal Sweet Talk

HIPPOS "Remember the Nile and our first date . . . ?
I *love* the way you've put on weight."

COWS "Elsie, you're my heart's content.
I love you more than . . . *two percent!*"

ARMADILLOS "I hear a love song, *Clankety-Clank*. . . .
Could that be you, my Valentank?"

PRAYING MANTISES "Why won't you stay, my honeybunch,
A little while? I'll make you . . . *lunch*."

BOA CONSTRICTORS "She loves me, she loves me not,
She loves me, she loves me . . . *knot!*"

PORCUPINES "Oh, Lancelot, we'd make great neighbors—
Not to mention little sabers!"

SKUNKS "Without you, Whiff, I wouldn't know
Which way these sudden breezes blow."

CHEETAHS "She chases me and I chase her
At sixty-seven miles purr."

GARTER SNAKES "Where'd you get that suit of clothes,
My lovely little garden hose?"

FLEAS "I wear my heart upon my flea knee
Because it's *very* Valenteeny!"

Pull-a-Toe

The Bully beefy Butcher knows
Five little girls that pull their toes.
And when he tries to whack a few
Potato-toes for his beef stew,
The girls, though courteous and kind,
Will kick him in the never mind!

49 St. Patrick

I saw a Leprechaun today.
He said to me, "Me boy,
Has young St. Patrick passed this way,
Old Ireland's pride and joy?"

Said I, "And many a year it's been
Since Patrick passed away."
Said he, "So long as Earth is green,
St. Paddy's here to stay."

48 Lost in Austin

There was a poor Texan from Austin—
A city he always got lost in—
Who told his wife, "Dearie,
So much for your theory!
    Ignoring all signs
    But the telephone lines,
I'm now in a suburb of Boston!"

Salmon

Ambitious fish
of waterfalls
and streams,
she seems
to dream
only of bears
and what
must follow
at the shallow
end of living—
concluding with
the grieving,
the giving,
and the leaving
of new life,
that simple
but heroic act
of trying, trying . . .
dying.

46 Who's Afraid of the Number 13?

My sister has triskaidekaphobia,
    a fear of the number 13,
Not to mention that old mysophobia
    (she's squeaky about being clean!).
She's also a homichlophobian,
    afraid of the mist and the fog,
And a crybaby, too (cynophobian)—
    I'm afraid she's afraid of the dog!

Who knows why she's pluviophobic,
    afraid rain is going to hit her?
Last week she was ailurophobic—
    the neighbors' cat came up and bit her.
How silly! She's pteronophobic,
    afraid to be tickled by feathers,
And rattled by big (demophobia)
    crowds that are gathered together.

She covers her eyes when it's lightning
    (because she has astrapophobia),
And she finds thunder gruesomely frightening
    (technically tonitrophobia).
So to hide from it all (pantaphobia),
    she's a regular sleepyhead;
Thank goodness she's not clinophobic—
    she never fears going to bed!

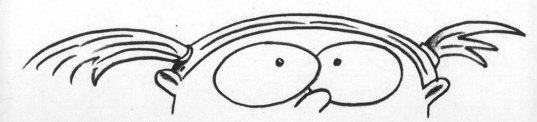

'Lo to the Buffalo, Hi to the Giraffe

It's sad to think that when you go
Across the plains the buffalo
Who's standing there—the one and only—
Is buffalone and buffalonely,

And sadder still to think that all
His cousin buffaloes we call
The wildebeests, from most to leastly,
Can be so awfully wildebeastly.

And have you wondered why the tall
Lumbering yellow beast we call
Giraffe must put up with shrill laughter
From birds who sit on her giraffter?

But oh by far the worst of all
Are Jungle cats whose fur can fall—
(Lions not the lionesses)—
In mainly manely tangled tresses.

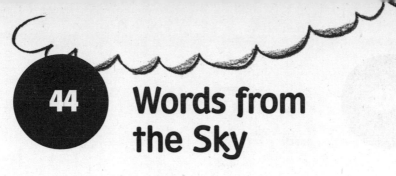

44 Words from the Sky

A buttercup of sun, said Sunday,
  Tipping his cap to the sky.

A slicker suit of rain, cried Monday,
  Sunday left me dry.

A whippersnapper wind, yelled Tuesday,
  Monday could not stay.

A marshmallow of cloud, sighed Wednesday,
  Tuesday's blown away.

A windowsill of snow, claimed Thursday,
  Wednesday had foretold.

An honesty of hail, called Friday,
  Thursday left me cold.

A funeral of fog, wept Saturday,
  Friday stung my eye.

A buttercup of sun, said Sunday,
  Tipping his cap to the sky.

43 April Fool's

They say you're the picture of pretty,
You're as warm as the heat from the sun,
You're the lock and the key to the city,
You're the beef in a hamburger bun!

They say you're the pick of the litter,
They say that you're such a good egg!
But, kid, have you stopped to consider
Someone might be pulling your leg?!

42 Animals at Odds

I

The snails and whales formed a committee
    To stamp out all extremes.
They set the rules in the low tide pools,
    And now they're at odds, it seems.

II

The pachyderms play tricks on worms
    And the worms, they wonder why.
The reason should be obvious—
    They can't see eye to eye.

III

When crested newts and bandicoots
    Play cards in the North Woolly Wood,
They hire a seal to cut and deal,
    And clap when he thinks he should.

Riddle

There was a boy from Whited,
Who had become excited
Because he'd been invited
To see a baseball game.

When everyone was seated,
The boy was warmly greeted.
Three letters I've repeated
Six times. What is his name?

ANSWER: Ted

Beneath a Shady Tree

Beneath a shady tree, they lay.
He handed her a sweet bouquet.
She handed him back his toupee,
    And on his head it rested.

He said, "For you, my Caroline,
I'll walk the straight and narrow line!"
But just above his hair-o-line,
    Two bobolinks had nested.

The Race

39

Have you always run faster than lightning
To the timekeeper's tape on the track?
    Were there footsteps like thunder
    That led you to wonder
If maybe you ought to look back?

Did you know your last kick at this distance
Was likely to lengthen your lead?
    Could you hear someone yelling,
    "The boy from New Welling-
ton Middle is picking up speed"?

Is that when you tested your courage
To tear at the top of the turn?
    When everyone finished,
    Their fires diminished,
They knew you had plenty to burn.

38 Ocean Motion

If you hear the Ocean weeping
  In a seashell by the shore,
It is dreaming while it's sleeping
  On its bed, the Ocean floor.

If you see the Ocean waving
  Wildly along the shore,
It is simply misbehaving
  Like it's always done before.

37 In the Garden of Eden

Well, he liked her
And she liked him.
He was proper,
She was prim.

And she liked him
And he liked her,
Until they met . . .
The Slitherer.

Old Names, New Names

36

Alice Springs was once called Sturt,
Australia. New names never hurt.

Peking, China, then Beiping,
Changed one letter—now Beijing!

Paris (born Lutetia, France)
Could go back? *Non*, not a chance.

Delhi, India, rightly claims
Half a dozen previous names.

In Turkey, Istanbul, I hope'll
Not be called Constantinople

Like before, or else become
Once again Byzantium.

Tokyo, Japan, was Edo,
Which they took a vote to veto.

Used to call Regina (Sask.)
Pile o' Bones (you had to ask?).

Names are like new pairs of shoes—
They wear out and then we choose

Another pair we think might fit
Once we get the hang of it.

35 Moon Candy

One plum-dark night, a crazy kid
Found one white jelly bean. The jar
Jiggled as he unscrewed the lid.
He threw the jelly bean so far
It hit the moon, as in a dream,
And shot to earth . . . a jelly beam.

34 Spirit of the Seder

Our house is cleansed, and we await
The celebration of the eight
Days of Pesach. Girl and boy
Anticipate the feast of joy.

Once again we praise the giver,
Whose Gift of Gifts was to deliver
Us from ancient bondage, chains
That scarred the parched Egyptian plains.

Leave no family on its own
To celebrate this feast alone:
Invite them all to see and hear it;
Share the freedom of the spirit.

Easter Is . . .

the lily Aunt Mamie used to wear.
a breath of fresh air.
the mayor's wife riding in the motorcade.
Uncle Pete, who visited last year—and stayed.
St. Cosmo's, where folks line up outside.
a day so fine the sun's ashamed to hide.
spring, exaggerated.
a purple hard-boiled egg . . . I ate it.

32 Acrobats

There lives an old man at the tip end of town.
He's the once famous trapeze and carnival clown
Who spent the best part of his life upside down—
    He jokes about his higher calling.

He sits on his porch with his dog, Gunga Din,
And he talks of his aerial act with his twin—
How they'd tumble and tremble and spiral and spin,
    A matter of inches from falling.

And he tells me how people would come to the fair
For the chance to see acrobats climbing the air,
And to holler and hoot—or to shout up a dare,
    While elephants went on parading.

How can I recapture the time of our time—
The Flying Danisovich Twins *in their prime—*
When yesterday's pictures keep coming, but I'm,
    Like all of them, hopelessly fading.

What's left of the ladies and gents in the stands,
The Big Top, the nets, or the high-flying plans?
Only the memory . . . my brother's soft hands
    Apart in the sudden air . . . waiting.

If The Earth Bumps the Moon

A Bedtime Lullaby

Moon, if you and Stars should blink,
What on Earth would Heaven think?

Earth, if you get bumped by Moon,
Will it burst our blue balloon?

Sun, if you and Moon collide,
Who will turn the evening tide?

Moon, if you eclipse the Sun,
How can Noon have any fun?

Sky, if Rainbow paints the air . . . ,
Multicolored Thunderwear?

Wind, if you should spank the rain . . . ,
Tears upon my windowpane.

Dark, when you turn off the Day . . . ,
I was sleepy anyway.

Moon, if you begin to weep,
Night will rock me back to sleep.
Night will rock me back to sleep.

31

Autograph Verses

You're my saucer, I'm your dish,
You're my wishbone, I'm your wish.
You're my peanut, I'm your butter.
You're my flag, I'm all aflutter.

★ ★

I like my ice cream cones vanilla,
I like my envelopes manila,
I like my animals gorilla,
I like cute girls like you,
      PRISCILLA!

★ ★

H_2O is water,
CaO is lime,
NaCl is salt,
YoU are mine.

★ ★

I love you, honey, come what may
From Maine to South Dakota,
But do you think there's any way
Not to slurp your soda?

Between the Uprights?

It's 21-20 with 6 ticks left, plenty of time for "Big Foot" Nelson to put

R O O S E V E L T

High on top of the Lions, the League, the State, the clouds. The crowd's gone hush. Big Foot hikes his pants, plants his nick-name in the mud. The count, the snap, the THUD! The goal posts divide. It's, it's, it's . . . **WIDE!**

Ars Libri
after Archibald MacLeish

A book should be spirited and odd
As a divining rod,

Wild
As the wonder of a child,

Open to the sky and the slanting rain
As an attic's shattered windowpane.

A book should measure its success
By a censor's distress.

★ ★

A book should be ten candle-watts
Of afterthoughts,

Brilliant as a marbled vein in a quarry
Of story,

Bold enough to leave behind
Unpeace of mind.

A book should be a welcome late-night guest
After a day-long standardized test.

★ ★

A book should be the map, flashlight, and skeleton key
To literacy.

For all imaginations out of whack or work,
The CEO and the filing clerk,

For kids
Who yearn to see but hesitate to dream—

A book should both be
And seem.

27

Leaving Small Town America

The day we moved away it rained
  And rained and rained some more.
The town grew famous after that,
  Though I forget what for.

It had a candy shop, *Sweet Dreams*,
  Beside a waterfall,
A grocery store, two restaurants,
  One doctor. That was all.

But we stayed on, inventing hours
  Each ordinary day.
All I remember is it rained
  The day we moved away.

26 Fire Dog

Up out of bed
They hit the hole,
Ten firemen sliding
Down the pole.

They climb aboard
The big machine,
The reddest red
You've ever seen.

The siren screams,
The engine roars.
Some people watch
From open doors

A rainbow curve
Across the lawn.
The chief keeps shouting,
"Pour it on!"

A quiet statue's
Standing by—
The spotted dog
With one black eye.

The Whitest White

What is the whitest white you know?
A ghost, an angel, drifting snow,
Lightning, lilies, a sun-washed stone?
That winter you were lost, alone?

What's whiter than a cup of flour?
A seagull? Death at the dying hour?
A tortoise egg, sea salt, a sheet
Unwinding in the wind? White heat?

Or something you might easily miss—
A page out of a book

                              . . . like this.

24 The Kentucky Derby

Hugging the clubhouse turn,
Whipping along the rail,
The wind at Churchill Downs
Picks up the pace to sail

With Whirlaway, Citation,
Gallant Fox, Seattle Slew,
Swaps, or Secretarial—
The pack comes into view.

And as they turn for home
Four-leggeds feel the crack-
ling whip hand of the wind
Racing around the track,

But let the records show,
Of all the Triple Crowns,
The wind has never won
A Place at Churchill Downs.

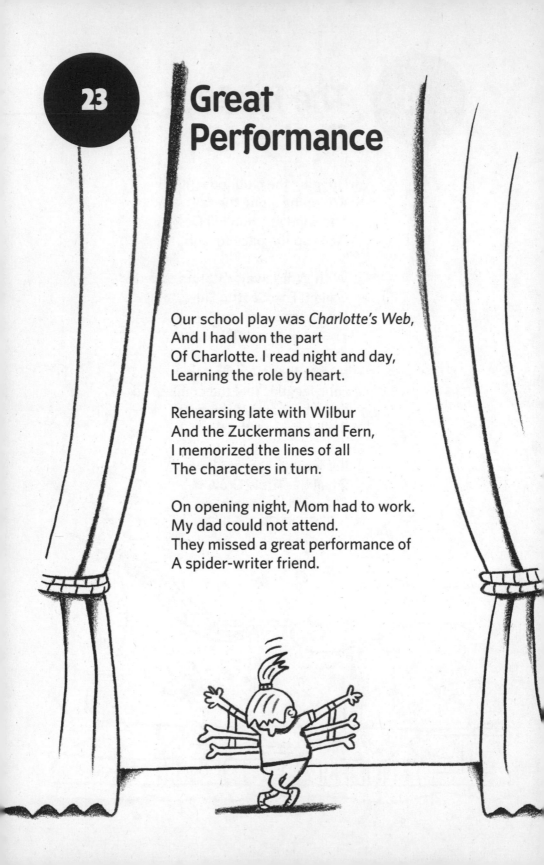

23 Great Performance

Our school play was *Charlotte's Web*,
And I had won the part
Of Charlotte. I read night and day,
Learning the role by heart.

Rehearsing late with Wilbur
And the Zuckermans and Fern,
I memorized the lines of all
The characters in turn.

On opening night, Mom had to work.
My dad could not attend.
They missed a great performance of
A spider-writer friend.

The Feather Duster

Buster, Buster, feather duster,
Had a maid but couldn't trust her.
She said she would clean the cupboard.
"Buster, first things first," she blubbered.
So to get a brilliant luster,
She continued scrubbing Buster.

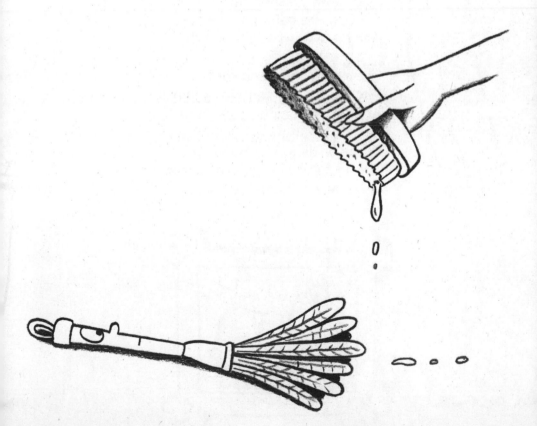

Famous Civil War Horses

Some were small, some overgrown,
Black or dapple gray or roan,
Fitted out for the battle zone.

Traveler honored Lee's advance.
Cincinnati measured Grant's
Step for step with circumstance.

Baldy cantered under Meade,
Hooker's Lookout took the lead
Like a fine and prominent steed.

Blackhawk, Slasher, Almond Eye,
Old Fox, Fire-eater galloped by.
And there was Little Sorrel shy,

Like a pony short and slim.
"Stonewall" Jackson, riding him
At Chancellorsville, lost a limb

Before he died. Second to none,
The horse was like a favorite son
In war as pivotal as the gun.

The Eyefull Tower

```
                    M
                    o
                    n
                  cher-
                ie, c'est
                P a r e e!
                 Wowwow
                 Wowwoww
               oOu-la-la!w
               owowwowwow
               wowwowowwwo
              wwowwowwowwo
              wwowwowwowwow
             owBonjour, madame!
            Wowwowwowwowwowow
            Wowwowwowwowwowowo
           wwowwMagnifique!owwo
           owwowwowwowwowwowow
          wowowwowwowwowwowwoww
         wowwowwowwowwowwowwowwow
        wowwowwowwowwowwowwowwowwow
         wowwowwowwowwowwowwowwowwow
        wowwowwowwowwowwowwowwowwow
       wowwowwowwowwowwowwowowwowoww
       owwowwowwowwowwowwowwowwowwowwo
      wwowwowwowwowwowwowwowwowwowwowwo
      wwowwowwowwowwowwowwowwowwowwowwo
     wwowwowwowwowwowwowwowwowwowwowwowwo
     w w o w w o w w o w w o w w o w w o w Oui! Oui! Oui!w o w w w o w
    wowwowwowwowwowwowwowwowwowwowwowwowwowwowwow
    owwowwowwowwowwowwowwowwowwowwowwowwowwowowwoww
   owwowwowwowwowwowwowwowwowwowwowwowwowwowwowwow
   wowwowwowwowwowwowwowwowwowwowwowwowwwowwowwoww
   owwowwowwowwowwowwowwowwowwowwowowwowwowwwowwoww
  owwowwowwowwowwowwowwowwowwowwowwowwowwowwwowwoww
  owwowwowwowwowwowwowwowwowwowwowwowwowwwowwowwowwo
 owwowwowwowwowwowwowwowwowwowwowwoL'ENTRÉEowwowwowwowwowwowwowwowwowwo
```

19 Ding-a-Ling, the Dragon

A sensitive young dragon once could not recall his name.
He tried, he tried so hard, but he could not recall his name.

"I could be Isaac Newt," said he, "or the Scarlet Pimpernel!
The Prince of Warts? Or Prickleback?" No name would ring a bell.

Dear Lizards
(went the letter to his cousins),

Don't you see?!
I'm a sensitive young Dragon,
here's a photograph of me.
So if you've got a minute,
and if you've got a clue,
write to me immediately!

Sincerely,
Dragon Who?

By truckloads came the telegrams with bushels of advice.
And some were rather personal but all were very nice.

A Dragon Lady sent a short but sympathetic note—
"Dear Ding-a-ling the Dragonboy . . ."
And that was all she wrote.

For Dragonboy remembered . . . . every lizard heard him yell!
"I'm Ding-a-ling, Ding-ding-a-ling!" Which finally rang a bell.

18 Postcard

Arnold wrote you two novellas,
Deion wrote you one short story.
What you get from this here fella's
Short and self-explanatory.

Love, J.P.

Impossible Mom

17

Does your mother take you to soccer games
   When your dad's too sick to go?
Does she search the Internet for your
   Report on Geronimo?
Does she help you with arithmetic
   Too difficult to learn?
Does she eat the chocolate cake you made
   With the oven set on "**burn**"?
Does anyone else give you quite as much
   Of the benefit of the doubt?
Does she understand a kid's entitled
   To throw a fit and pout?
Does she get dressed up at holiday time—
   A *ridiculous* Santa's elf?
Amazing to think your mother was once
   An impossible kid herself!

16 **Susie's Juicy Sushi**

Sue saw sushi
On her shoe, see?
She set sushi
In a stew. She
Called it "Susie's
Juicy Stewshi."

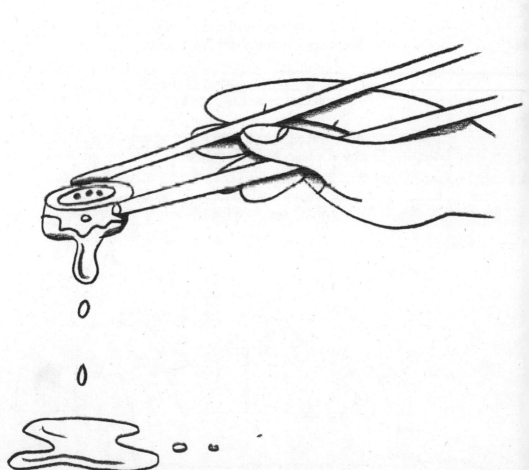

15 Betelgeuse, the Star

Here's a startling bit of news:
See that star called Betelgeuse,

A star about a thousand times
As big as ours, the sun? It climbs

The dark infinity of night
And switches on its reddish light,

Which travels fast but seems so slow
Because, five hundred years ago,

Its brilliant candlepower from birth
Took all that time to get to Earth.

And that's the startling bit of news:
Orion's favorite, Betelgeuse,

Is shining down. Despite the wait,
Its light arrives . . . a little late.

The Hangman Shouts a One-Word Poem

NECKST!

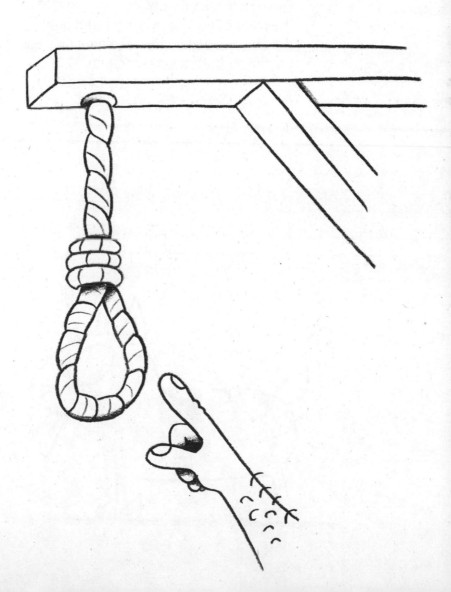

13 Violet Is . . .

my cat's tongue
lavender out on a holiday
blush pears
bruised peaches
pain gone away
Earth from six miles high
the color of my dreams after midnight
the afternoon glancing off a grackle's back
the flower that bears her name

12 The Double Bogey Man

Double bogey Delmore Duff
Punished his clubs when the roughs got rough.
Hacked at weeds and whacked that wood
Till it sailed into the neighborhood!
Smacked the ball with an iron somehow—
It beaned a horse,
Frightened a cow,
Bounced off a barn
And a green Mustang,
Before it began to boomerang!
Delmore Duff
Was checking his score . . .
That's what the Bogey Man's out here—

FORE!

A Horizontal Tale

At the hot construction site—
A hundred fifteen Fahrenheit!—
Here is how the story goes:
Stevie took off all his clothes.

Bulldozer rolled Stevie—*splat!*
He reappeared in nothing. Flat.

The Most Common Vowel

The vowel "a," as in star or watch,
is found in every language.

Isn't it awfully
nice to know
that no matter
where you go,
Timbuktu or Tokyo,
Istanbul or Arkansas,
everybody's saying

"Ahhhh"?

"Ah" can mean
so many things—
"Aunt Bertha's nose"
or "wigs for kings,"
"late last night,"
"thirteen plus four,"
or "Lester, dear,
please shut the door!"

People talking
blah blah blah
always end up saying,

"Ahhhh."

The Buzz About Mrs. Shakespeare

Mrs. Shakespeare, what a gal!
She said, "William, my pen pal,
How would you like twins next year?"
William sighed, "How lovely, dear."

Later, humming in their pram,
Judith (Jude) and Hamnet (Ham),
Caused a most peculiar buzz.
Mom confused them as it was—

Called them Honey One and Two.
What could Ham and Judy do?
Said to William, "Papa, please,
Are we two bees or not two bees?"

A Banana Is

A
yel-
low
long-
fel-
low
pack-
age
deal
that
has a
very
slip-
pery
ap-
p
e
a
l

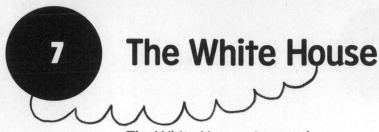

The White House

The White House sits on a lawn
Under an emerald tree.
The people are hanging on
To see what there is to see.

As long as a soldier guard
Stands by the entranceway,
Whoever steps into the yard,
Whatever the time of day,

The people from Anywhere,
So near to a brush with fame,
Tiptoe, point fingers, stare,
And whisper the person's name.

American days go by.
The White House is never far,
A vision, like Versailles,
Wherever the people are.

The Ancient Princess

My age? I've forgotten. I must look a sight—
  My body has shriveled to prunes.
What little I've left of my hair has turned white
  And I can't tell the forks from the spoons.

I used to be known as the Belle of the Balls
  When I batted my eyes at the Prince.
But my winters have ruined my frolicsome falls—
  I haven't caught sight of him since.

Age is but a word, not the end of the road,
  And it doesn't take much, as you see,
To feel like a princess (but look like a toad)
  With the other toads taking high tea.

We laugh at the past, oh the memory sings
  With lighthearted days of our youth.
We whisper outrageously mischievous things—
  And every so often, the truth.

Epitaph for a Catcher

Here lies Nick "No-Knees" McGirk,
Squatted when he went to work,
Squatted when he went to bed,
Squatting now that he is dead.
His casket's only half the size
Of any other normal guy's
Because, no taller than an elf,
Mick could not unsquat himself.

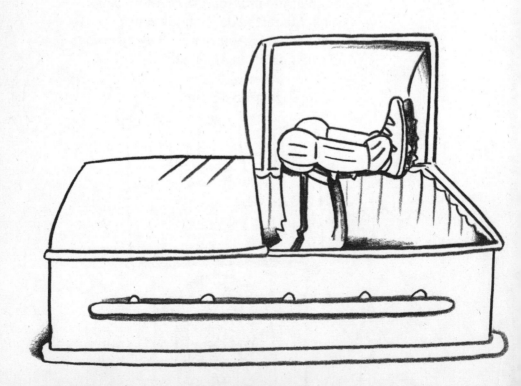

4 Water Haiku

A wallop of whale!
Waves lapping at the ankles
of Oregon

* *

Chill waters—
an S of eel,
a V of piranha—
electric moment!

* *

Ocean liner gone . . .
the minnows get on
with their important lives

* *

An otter water-
toboggans over and down
the backside of life

Sleep Day

If I were my father and this were my day,
What kind of day would it be?
A grand-slam home-run day,
Grilled-hamburger-bun day,
A place-in-the-sun day for me.

If I were my father, and this were my day,
I'd make it the best day yet.
A splash-in-the-pool day,
A break-every-rule day,
A too-super cool day? You bet.

But I'm not my dad,
So I have to put on
My Father's Day thinking cap.
A whopping-big-fish day?
A genie-three-wish day?
No. All my dad wants is a nap.

2 Oops!

I put a frog inside her lunchbox
And slid a slug inside her desk
And slipped a spider in her jacket,
And weird stuff equally grotesque.
She shouted, "Patrick, thanks a lot
For sharing this disgusting creature!"

The moral: You had better not
Scare a friend if she's your Teacher.

School's Out!

School is out and I'm so sad
(That is what I told my dad).
I'll miss Mrs. Rosenbaum
(That is what I told my mom).
I'd keep going but I can't
(That is what I told my aunt).
Homework helps me stay awake
(That is what I told my snake).
Room 13 is where it's at
(That is what I told the cat).
Tests are over—what a bummer.
This'll be a boring summer.
School is out and I feel lost.
(It's hard keeping your fingers crossed!)